A Giant Step for Andy

Take the 't' out of I can't and turn it into 'I can'!

Diana Jean La Fontaine

Written by
Diana Jean La Fontaine

Illustrated by
Tracey Taylor Arvidson

To Rich – Thank you for your unwavering encouragement and belief in me. To my sons, Chris and Kevin, make pursuing your dreams part of your present. There are many unexpected gifts to discover along the way. As well, my gratitude to my mom who lovingly read many inspiring books to me when I was very young. A GIANT thank you to the kiddos at Tobler ES.

DJL

For Molly

TTA

ISBN-13: 978-1500696986

ISBN-10: 1500696986

Andy was wild about elephants.

His bedroom was filled with a herd of toys, books, and drawings all having to do with elephants.

But of all the elephant treasure Andy had, his favorite was a snuggly, worn, stuffed elephant he called Oliphant. Andy took him mostly everywhere he went. Oliphant was Andy's faithful friend.

When Andy arrived home from
school each day, he would sit in his room
drawing pictures of elephants with Oliphant
at his side instead of playing outside with the other
kids in the neighborhood. Like many kids with autism,
Andy had difficulty meeting people and making new friends.

Sometimes, though, Andy wished he had a pal to play with him . . . and Oliphant.

Each morning, come rain or shine, when Andy got out of bed, he marked the day on his calendar with an "X" to count down the days to Saturday.

Saturday was the most important day of the week because that's when he and his dad would visit the elephants at the zoo.

"Andy!" called out his dad. "It's Saturday! Time to get up and get dressed."

Andy jumped out of bed, fluttering his hands with excitement.

"Hurrah! It's zoo day!" he shouted and followed that with the trumpeting sound he called elephant talk. "I'm ginormously happy!" he said, tossing Oliphant up in the air.

"That's a clever word," said his dad.

"That's *giant* and *enormous* put together. Just like an elephant."

Then Andy grabbed his gray crayon and drew a little elephant in the square under Saturday on his calendar.

Andy quickly put on his
favorite striped shirt, khaki shorts,
safari jacket, and his backpack.
Then he waited by the front
door with Oliphant in tow.

"Did you brush your teeth?" his dad asked.

Andy shook his head no. "I'm letting my
incisor teeth grow into tusks!" he declared.
"Brushing wears them down."

"Boys can't grow tusks." His dad grinned. "Now go brush
your teeth!"

Andy slowly marched up the stairs, stomping his
feet like a pachyderm. "I bet elephants don't have to brush their
teeth!" he complained to Oliphant.

While Andy and Oliphant rode in the car to the zoo, Andy daydreamed that he was on safari in Africa. He imagined his dad's car was a rusty old Jeep roaming its way over the bumpy trails and through tall brush to find a herd of elephants.

What an adventure!

Once at the zoo, Andy pulled his dad along by the hand.

"If only my feet had wheels," said his dad, stumbling to keep up.

Andy stopped short. Confused, he looked up at his dad. "Feet can't have wheels," he protested. "How would your shoes fit if your feet had wheels?"

But Andy didn't wait for an answer. He'd already spied the elephants in the distance.

When Andy got close enough, he let go of his dad's hand. He ran past the crowd toward the railing to get a better look.

Kids in the crowd were **shouting** to get the elephant's attention.

Loud noises bothered Andy, so he plugged his ears with his thumbs and began to hum.

As soon as he relaxed, he forgot all about the noise and watched one of the elephants get a bath with a zookeeper's hose.

Another zookeeper spotted Andy in his safari jacket, and she walked over to greet him. "Are you our new elephant handler?" she asked.

Andy didn't look at her. His dad moved his thumbs away from his ears, and the zookeeper repeated her question. But Andy just kept watching the elephant.

The zookeeper looked puzzled. She didn't know that Andy felt uncomfortable talking to new people.

"Hi, my name is Don, and this is my son, Andy," his dad greeted her. "Andy is usually quiet until he gets to know you."

The zookeeper smiled. "My name is Nancie," she said. "It's nice to meet you both."

Andy's dad bent down and whispered in Andy's ear, "Please say hi to Nancie."

Andy looked toward Nancie's feet, but then he quickly looked back at the elephant.

"It's hard for Andy to focus on anything but the elephant right now," explained his dad.

"I understand. I give the elephants all my attention, too. Well, Andy, enjoy the elephants," said Nancie as she walked away.

Saying hi to people gave Andy the jitters. He just couldn't understand why it was so important. When he felt nervous, his skin would get itchy. He'd scratch at his arms and pull at his shirt. It felt like ants were crawling under his clothes!

"Andy, it's important to be polite. When you ignore people, it can make them feel bad," his dad reminded him.

With a frown, he said to his dad, "I can't."

Andy was frustrated. He just wanted to be left alone to watch the elephants. The gentle giants made him feel calmer. With his dad close behind him, he moved down the railing in search of his favorite elephant, Tusker.

Andy

climbed

onto

a

big

rock beside the railing. From there, he could view the
entire elephant camp.

First, Andy saw Peanut, the littlest elephant. She liked to stand in place, swinging her trunk back and forth like a dance.

Off in a corner was Einstein, the busiest of the bunch. He collected sticks to use as backscratchers to get to the difficult-to-reach spots.

Tusker was on the far left eating from a hanging barrel of straw. He was a mountainous African elephant with ivory tusks as long as Andy was tall and ears the size of a mammoth kite.

As Andy watched, a blue jay perched itself on Tusker's back to peck at the straw that fell on the big elephant's head. Tusker didn't seem to mind sharing his food.

They must be friends, Andy thought.

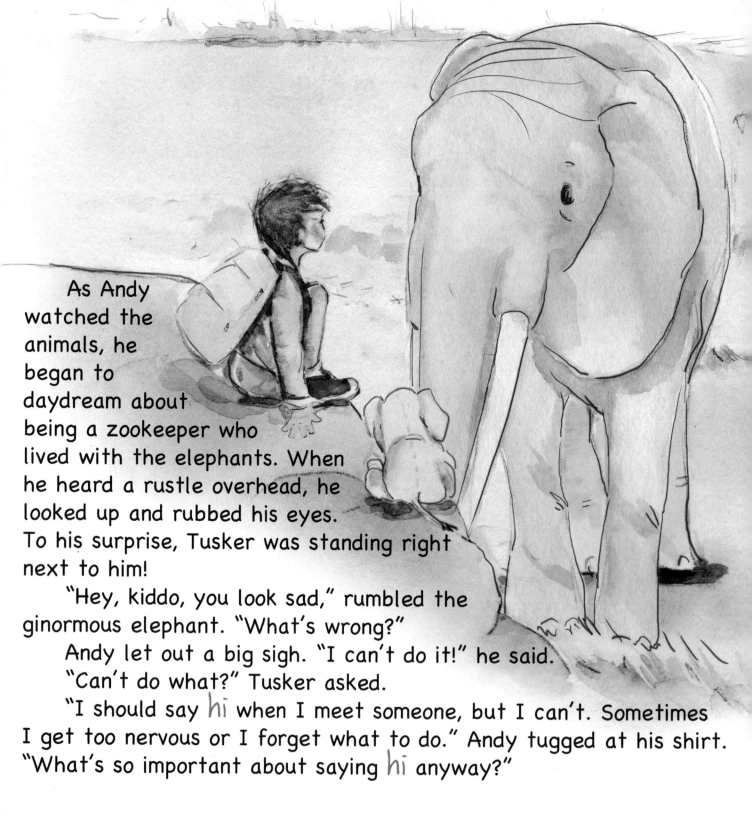

As Andy watched the animals, he began to daydream about being a zookeeper who lived with the elephants. When he heard a rustle overhead, he looked up and rubbed his eyes. To his surprise, Tusker was standing right next to him!

"Hey, kiddo, you look sad," rumbled the ginormous elephant. "What's wrong?"

Andy let out a big sigh. "I can't do it!" he said.

"Can't do what?" Tusker asked.

"I should say hi when I meet someone, but I can't. Sometimes I get too nervous or I forget what to do." Andy tugged at his shirt. "What's so important about saying hi anyway?"

"Nobody wants to feel like they are being ignored," explained Tusker.

"Everyone wants to feel welcome, including you, kiddo."

Andy crossed his arms and looked away. "I can't."

"Kiddo, I'm going to help you take the 't' out of 'I can't' and turn it into 'I can,'" Tusker told him.

Andy listened closely to what the elephant had to say.

"I understand how you feel. When I was young, I had to learn how to talk to other calves at the waterhole."

"You did?" Andy asked.

"Sure, we all have to learn social skills, even elephants," Tusker said. "I'll teach you how to introduce yourself to someone new. This skill will help you feel more comfortable saying hi to people and even make new friends."

Andy liked the idea.

"First, you have to learn the basic steps," Tusker explained. "Then you have to *practice* the steps again and again until you can do it without thinking about it, until it becomes *natural*."

Tusker trumpeted for Peanut to join them.

Feeling nervous yet excited to meet the littlest elephant, Andy forgot to say hi. Instead, he began telling Peanut about his stuffed friend, Oliphant.

As Andy was about to begin his next sentence, Peanut put the tip of her trunk in his open mouth.

Andy jumped back and hid beside Tusker.

"*ptooey, ptooey, blech!*," Andy protested.

"Peanut was just saying hello to you," Tusker explained. "Elephants greet each other by touching trunks. That's how we get a *taste* of who others are."

"Well, that tasted like dirty socks!" Andy cried out. He didn't stop to think that his words might hurt Peanut's feelings.

Peanut swayed her head sadly.

Tusker trumpeted, "It's okay Andy, you didn't know how elephants say hi to each other."

Peanut looked at Andy. "I didn't mean to upset you. Can we start over?" she squeaked.

"Peanut, we are going to teach Andy how to introduce himself the way people do," Tusker explained. "You will play the part of Nancie, the zookeeper. And kiddo, you will play yourself."
Then, clearing his throat, the big elephant said with importance, "And \ will be the director."

Feathers, the blue jay, flew over from a nearby tree and landed on Tusker's tusk. "What will I be?" she chirped.
"The silent audience," Tusker directed with a chuckle, causing Feathers to puff up her chest and flap her wings unhappily. "Okay, okay, you can be my assistant," he roared.

Tusker grabbed a leafy branch with his trunk and cleared a spot for a stage. He explained to Andy that when Peanut says hello to him, he would need to stop, look at her, and listen. Feathers helped by going over the directions with Andy and Peanut.

When Tusker felt the pair was ready, he used his trunk like a megaphone: "Lights, camera, action!"

Lights camera action

Peanut walked up to Andy. "Hi, my name is Nancie."

Andy felt uneasy and looked down at Oliphant and repeated quietly, "Hi, my name is Nancie."

"Cut!" Tusker called out, ears flapping. "That was a good first try.

However, remember to

stop,

look,

and

listen,

and then say **YOUR** part."

Feathers went over the lines with Andy and Peanut once more. When she signaled that they were ready, Tusker called out, "Take two, and . . . action!"

Peanut said her line, but Andy just stood there looking at his feet.

Feathers flew onto Andy's shoulder and whistled, "Hi, my name is—"
Andy clenched his fists. "I can't do it!"
Peanut patted Andy's back with her trunk. "I used to get confused about how to greet other elephants, but I kept on trying."
Tusker agreed. "That's right. Social skills take practice, kiddo."
"Just relax. You can learn the steps," whistled Feathers.
Andy felt encouraged by his friends to try again, and he did.

Andy and Peanut continued to practice their lines, and each time Andy played his part, it became easier to remember what to say and do.

Tusker raised his trunk to give Andy a high-five. "Give it here, kiddo. The rehearsal is going well. Let's take a break. You earned it!"

Andy felt happy.

"Follow me to my favorite play area," Peanut invited him, and Andy took hold of her tail, feeling his heart beat fast with excitement.

When Feathers called for the two to come back, Andy and Peanut began practicing their parts again. Feathers reminded Andy of the three important steps.

When Tusker called out Action!, Andy stopped and looked at Peanut as she approached him. He listened when she introduced herself. Then he replied, "Hi, my name is Andy."

Everyone cheered.

"I did it!" Andy shouted happily, and he hugged Tusker's leg. "I DID IT!"

"See, you *can* do it, kiddo!" Tusker said proudly. "Keep practicing at home with your family because the more you practice, the easier it will get!"

Andy agreed. He put Oliphant into his backpack and climbed off the rock.

Andy ran over to his dad, who was seated on a nearby bench.

"I was playing and talking with the elephants!" sang Andy. "And Tusker taught me how to say hi and introduce myself to a new friend!"

"He did?" Andy's dad smiled. "Tell me all about it."

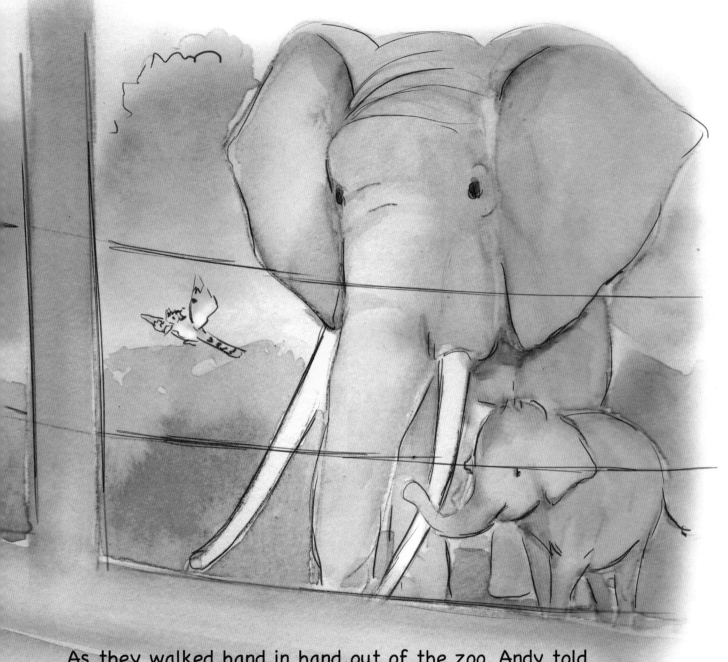

As they walked hand in hand out of the zoo, Andy told his dad all about how he had learned to stop, look, and listen.

The following Saturday when Andy and his dad arrived back at the zoo, Andy saw the zookeeper walking by.

He looked at her and called out, "Hi!"

Nancie waved and shouted back, "Hi, Andy, nice to see you!"

Andy smiled at his dad and cheered. "I did it. I looked at her and said hi, just like we practiced!"

Andy's dad hugged him. "I knew you could do it, kiddo," he said.

Andy climbed onto the rock to share the good news with Tusker.
"Way to go, kiddo! I can tell you have been practicing. You can do it!" the elephant trumpeted.

Andy hands fluttered as he cheered. "I can do it!"

Einstein looked over at the pair when he heard the excitement. Tusker called him over.

When Einstein got close, Andy said, "Hi, I'm Andy."

"Hi, I'm Einstein. Good to meet you, Andy. Oh, grab that stick and scratch behind my ear, please."

Andy was glad to help his new elephant friend.

"Awesome! You've really got it," said Tusker. "How can I reward you for your hard work?"

Andy knew within a second. "I'd like a ride on your back!"

Tusker bent down, and Andy climbed up. "Gee whiz, I'm as **TALL** as a mountain!" he shouted.

As Tusker strolled along, he said, "Now that you know how to say hi and introduce yourself to new people, you'll make more friends."

"But what if I forget or get nervous?" Andy whispered into the ginormous ear.

Tusker rumbled, "Think like an elephant, and you'll never forget. If you get nervous, just relax and you'll remember."

Up there on Tusker's back,
Andy felt like he was on top
of the world. And when he climbed
down, he felt happy because he
had learned his first social
skill and to say I can
instead of I can't.

He gave Tusker a big hug. "You are my friend."
Tusker smiled as he cleared his throat. "Now remember
to stop, look, and listen."
"Okay, Tusker, I can!"

Andy and his dad headed over to the playground. Andy stood by the slide with Oliphant.

"Hi," said a soft voice next to him. Stop, look, and listen, Andy thought to himself.

So he stopped, turned to look at who was talking, and then listened to the girl standing beside him.

"My name is Savannah," she said.

"Hi, I'm Andy!" he replied.

Savannah smiled. "Do you want to play on the elephant slide?"

Andy raced over to his dad.
"Can I play with Savannah?"
he asked.

"Absolutely!" said his dad. "You can!"
"I can!" Andy shouted to Savannah.
Andy was about to run off when he stopped and placed Oliphant onto his dad's lap. "Take care of Oliphant for me. I'm going to play with my new friend!"
"Way to go, kiddo!" said his dad.
Andy gave his dad a high-five before running off to play.

Made in the USA
Charleston, SC
14 September 2014